the Milo Adventures

MILO AND ONE DEAD ANGRY DRUID

Mary Arrigan studied at the National College of Art, Dublin, and at Florence University. She became a fulltime writer in 1994. Her latest novel for teenagers, *The Rabbit Girl*, one of her forty-two published books, was selected by The United States Board of Books for Young People on their list of Outstanding International Books for 2012. Her awards include the International White Ravens title (Munich), a Bisto Merit Award, *The Sunday Times* Crime Writers Association Award and The Hennessy Short Story Award. Her books have been translated into twelve languages.

THE MILO ADVENTURES

MILO AND ONE DEAD ANGRY DRUID

WRITTEN AND ILLUSTRATED BY

MARY ARRIGAN

THE O'BRIEN PRESS
DUBLIN

First published 2013 by The O'Brien Press Ltd.,
12 Terenure Road East, Rathgar, Dublin 6, Ireland.
Tel: +353 1 4923333; Fax: +353 1 4922777
E-mail: books@obrien.ie
Website: www.obrien.ie

ISBN: 978-1-84717-351-5

1 2 3 4 5 6 7 8 9 10
13 14 15 16 17

Layout and design: The O'Brien Press Ltd.
Cover illustrations: Neil Price
Printed and bound by CPI Group (UK) Ltd, Croydon, CR0 4YY
The paper in this book is produced using pulp from
managed forests.

The O'Brien Press receives assistance from

Love and thanks to my husband, Emmet,
for his patient help and great cuisine.

This book was inspired by a visit to a big house
near Roscrea in County Tipperary. The eccentric
gentleman who once lived there alone would
pay local farmers four pence each for any
unusual shaped rocks or stones. My thanks to
Mary Dempsey and family for showing me this
extraordinary collection in their garden.

CONTENTS

CHAPTER ONE

SOMETHING OLD

On that Tuesday, when our teacher Miss Lee said that we were all to bring something old to school and talk about it, Shane stood up and said that he'd bring something totally amazing. The class laughed and said, 'Oh, yeah?'

And he said, 'Sure. Just you wait.'

So everyone laughed again. Well, everyone except me. That was because Shane was my best mate. He lived at the end of my road with his gran, Big Ella, who painted big splashy paintings in mad colours. She said Ireland needed sunshiny colours on account of all the grey rain.

Shane's clothes were way too small for him because he was a bit of a roly-poly, addicted to jammy donuts, squishy marshmallows and crisps. And yes, he did munch them all together.

Whenever anyone sniggered at his wobbly tummy, he'd just say that his chest had slipped a bit – like Obelix in my dad's old *Asterix* comics that Shane and I shared.

Nobody could make Shane angry. If his dark skin was pointed at by some idiot, he'd say he was 'well done' and not a 'half-baked porridge-face'. Everything was a laugh. Except if anyone made fun of his gran. That's when he'd roar like a bull and flatten them and then sit on them until they screamed. If they were smaller than him, that is.

Big Ella was the sort of person who made you feel glad to be with her. She was fun too, and I liked to visit her house because she was always either baking brilliant African lime cakes or painting big pictures, which she exhibited in the local art gallery.

Nobody knew what the pictures were about, not even if you looked sideways or stood on your head. So she didn't sell many, except maybe to someone who wanted to hide a damp wall or scare away intruders.

Sometimes Big Ella and Shane went away for days when she'd get a notion to paint some foggy mountain or windy lake. So, when they disappeared after the taking-something-old-to-school day, people just said what a nutter she was to take a young lad away from school. Nobody was worried. Except me. You see, I knew. And I was really scared.

CHAPTER TWO

A VERY WEIRD STONE

This is how it happened. On our way home from school that Tuesday afternoon, I asked Shane what was the amazing thing he was going to bring to the history class.

'You don't have anything at all,' I said. 'I know everything you have in your room, Shane, and you don't have anything interesting. It's all junk.'

'It's not in my room, Milo,' he grinned. 'I'll show you where it is. But if you tell anyone I'll drown you in sloppy cow-dung.'

I followed him through his gran's wild garden, to a bumpy area with piles of stones that were half hidden in the long grass.

'What are we coming here for?' I asked. 'There's nothing only grass and stones.'

'Not just *any* stones, Milo,' said Shane, stooping to pick one up. 'These were collected by Mister Lewis.'

'Who's Mister Lewis?' I asked.

'He lived in our house back in eighteen something-or-other,' explained Shane. 'He used to collect stones. Hundreds of them. He is supposed to have said that there was something special about the stones around here, so Gran says.'

'That's mental,' I laughed. 'Who'd want to collect stones?'

Shane shrugged. 'Well, he did. That's what Gran was told when she bought the house. I suppose people didn't have much to do back then.'

'What a saddo he was,' I hooted. 'Imagine – collecting stones!'

Shane pointed to the ground. 'Look,' he said. 'They were all buried here.'

'But these aren't buried,' I said, pointing to a pile of stones.

'They once were,' said Shane. 'Gran has been digging them up. She's going to build a studio here, and says she's damned if she's going to pay a builder to clear the site when she can do it herself. And me, of course,' he added. 'I get roped in to help.

You can help too, Milo.'

'So what's that got to do with the history stuff?' I asked, neatly side-stepping the 'help' word. 'This is just a load of grotty stones.'

'Not grotty,' retorted Shane, reaching into the pile and pulling up a stone shaped like a half moon. 'This one is really old.'

'All stones are old, Shane. Even you should know that. It takes millions of years to grow stones.'

'Ah, but this is different, Milo,' said Shane. 'Here, feel it.'

I took the stone. It was like a small broken wheel. On one side there was a pretty clear imprint of a fossil-ish thing.

'That's a prehistoric reptile,' said Shane. 'You can even see the scales. But that's not the best thing. Turn the stone over.'

I did, and gasped when I saw the pattern

of circles inside circles, just like the pattern on the huge stone outside the ancient burial place at Newgrange in County Meath. We'd gone there on a school outing once, and Miss Lee had told us that it was even older than the pyramids in Egypt. Shane said it was a pity they didn't have mummies and other dead stuff in there for a better atmosphere.

I touched the pattern. That was when I got the first strange feeling. My fingers tingled and a shiver went around my neck and shoulders. Shane was watching me and smiling.

'See? You feel it too. I bet you feel all shivery, don't you? Just like me and Gran did. She said that pattern was carved by Celts about three thousand years ago.'

'Yecch!' I said, thrusting the stone back

into his hands. 'You're one sicko. Do you know that? Making me hold something that dead people handled.'

Shane laughed. 'But they weren't dead when they carved it, you dope,' he said.

'I told you, Shane, all stones are ancient. Except for a few scratchy carvings on it, this looks just like any other.'

Shane shook his head. 'My gran says ...' he began.

'Shane!' I laughed. 'I love your gran, I do. But you do know she does mad arty stuff and talks to dandelions. Come on, mate, wise up. One of you has to stay sane.'

'Hey,' retorted Shane. 'That's Big Ella you're talking about, and she knows everything.'

'Well, I hope that's not your history thing, Shane,' I went on. 'It gives me the creeps.'

Shane grinned. 'Of course it's my history

thing,' he said. 'Who else will have something as amazing as this?'

I shivered again. But I didn't know why. Not then.

CHAPTER THREE

A LIZARD GOES MAD

We weren't supposed to bring living things to the history project. But Willie Jones swore his pet lizard never behaved badly, and that he'd only brought it because he said it just sat and did nothing in its special glass container, except doze on the pebbles and mini pond.

'Well, he is quiet all right,' said Miss Lee, holding up the container for all to see.

'Lizards have been around since prehistoric times,' said Willie, reading from a scrap of paper in case he'd forget the words. 'They taste and smell with their tongues. They know more than we think. It is said that they can predict strange things.'

'Maybe,' said Miss Lee. 'But I doubt it, looking at this lazy creature.'

'I looked it all up on Google,' said Willie. 'So it must be right.'

At my turn I was proud of my china cup. OK, the truth is I only thought of the bring-to-school thing that morning, so I nicked the cup from our kitchen dresser where Mum keeps stuff that's only used for people she wants to impress. The best part was making up a history story to go with it.

'It belonged to Grace O'Malley, the pirate queen,' I said, holding it up. 'She used to have tea-parties in her castle with her crew after their raids and that was the cup she drank from.'

Miss Lee took the cup and looked underneath. Then she smiled and pointed to the words on the bottom. *Made in Taiwan*.

'Eh, well,' I spluttered, frantically trying to come up with something intelligent (how is it that intelligence is never there when you need it)? 'There used to be a place called Taiwan in Ireland long ago,' I went on. 'It broke away from the west coast ... an earthquake smashed through it and it floated away ...' I was cut off by the yells of laughter.

'Very good, Milo,' Miss Lee said. 'Take good care of your – eh – precious pirate cup, and mind you don't pick up any swashbuckling habits from it.'

The rest of the class were still laughing as I made my way to my desk, trying to hide my face in my sweater.

'Now, Shane,' said Miss Lee. 'What do you have to show us?'

With a flourish like one of those magicians on TV, Shane took the stone from a Chinese takeaway bag. Everyone sniggered.

'A stone!'

'A lump of rock!'

'Way to go, big guy! WRONG way, ha–ha!'

But Miss Lee wasn't laughing. She stared at the carving. 'Where did you get this, Shane?' she asked.

But before Shane could answer, Willie Jones's lizard went mad. It began leaping about, scratching at the glass, trying to escape. And it did. While we were all shouting and crawling around the floor to catch it, our principal looked in to see what the noise was about. We all stopped and stared at her. Not because we were scared or anything, but we were always fascinated by her moustache and the way it wobbled when she was annoyed.

'Ss-sorry, Mrs Riley,' stuttered Miss Lee from the floor. 'Slight mishap with our history project.'

That was when the lizard made for the door. With a hairy shriek, Mrs Riley slammed the door and scarpered. Miss Lee got up and brushed her skirt and, once the lizard was safely back in his glass case, she made Willie put a heavy book over the top. Funnily enough, the lizard calmed down when Shane put the stone back into the bag.

Even though the rest of the class were still laughing, I got that strange, tingly feeling again.

'Shane,' said Miss Lee, 'You must mind that stone. In fact, there's one in the museum that looks just like it.' She reached out and took the stone from the bag again. 'Ask your granny where she ...' She broke off as the lizard went mad again.

On our way home from school, Shane was boasting. 'I told you this stone is special,' he said. 'Didn't I tell you Miss Lee would be impressed?'

'Dunno, Shane,' I muttered. 'It spooked me the way it made Willie's lizard go crazy.'

Shane laughed. 'It probably recognised its own great-great-multi-great-granddaddy carved on the back of my stone.'

I shivered. Could a stone be that powerful?

CHAPTER FOUR

AN INCIDENT WITH CRUNCH AND WEDGE

As we went through the school gates Shane stopped.

'Hey! I've a great idea, Milo. Let's go to the museum and see the stone that Miss Lee says is like mine.'

'Museum? It's not even raining, Shane!'

'Suit yourself,' said Shane. 'I'm going anyway. You coming?'

Well, I was curious – as you would be about a stone that drives a lazy lizard wild, so I decided to go along with Shane to see what all the fuss was about. But as we went around the corner into the alley that was a short cut to Main Street, we met trouble.

'Well, if isn't Fatman and Stick Insect. Goin' somewhere nice, eh?'

I groaned silently inside my head. This was all we needed – Crunch Kelly and Wedge Murphy from sixth class – whenever they actually came to school, that is. I know what you're thinking. You're thinking that those names were just any old made-up nicknames, but you'd be wrong. Kelly could really make your bones crunch and Murphy could wedge your underpants right up to your armpits. You get the picture? Not pleasant.

They stood in front of us, blocking our way, and Crunch patted Shane's tight, black curly hair. I clutched my schoolbag, ready to take a swing at them – and seeing the words 'death-wish' flashing in my mind. But it was Shane's takeaway bag that grabbed their attention.

'Hey, Crunch, look what we got here,' laughed Wedge, pointing to it. 'Takeaway! You hungry, Crunch? Me too. Hand it over, Fatman.'

Shane hugged the bag. 'It's not takeaway,' he muttered. 'It's a rock.'

'Yeah, right,' snarled Wedge. 'Like, you bring rocks around with you to eat, Fatman? When my good friend says to hand over your grub, you hand it over, OK?'

Then he snatched the takeaway bag from Shane – who did put up a bit of a fight, but we were like week-old jelly against these low-lifes. We watched with horror as they scarpered down the alley. I looked at my best mate, standing like a burst balloon and, with a surge of anger I belted off after those two like I was on fire, sparks shooting from my eyes.

I'd like to be able to say that I caught up with our attackers and beat THEM into week-old jelly, but the truth is that I found the bag thrown on the ground around the corner and the stone dumped a few yards farther on. So, they didn't fancy rock curry! I laughed with a whoosh of relief as I picked up the ancient tingly stone and put it back in the bag. Shane was puffing his way towards me. I held up the bag.

'You got it!' he stopped in eye-popping amazement.

'I did,' I laughed. 'I remembered my taekwon-do skills and sent them off with massive bruises.'

Shane took the bag and checked out the stone. 'Wow!' he said. 'You really did get it back, Milo.'

'Yep,' I stood up straight in macho-mode.

Then Shane looked at me with a sort of puzzled squint.

'Milo, you and me, we only lasted two Saturdays at junior taekwon-do when we were seven. And we were both rubbish and learnt nothing so how …?'

'OK, OK,' I said. 'So they threw it at me when they saw me coming at them with all guns blazing …'

Shane laughed and punched my shoulder.

'All right,' I muttered. 'So they threw it away when they found out it was really only a stone, but hey, I'm still the hero.'

CHAPTER FIVE

A SURPRISE IN THE MUSEUM

And so we went to the museum on the corner of Main Street and Chapel Lane. It had once been a posh town house, but in the mid-eighteen hundreds the family went back to England. Dad said it was the rain, boredom and the constant diet of bacon and watery cabbage that drove them away.

'Besides,' he went on, 'the shortage of other gentry around here meant they had only one another to talk to. There are only so many ways you can talk to the same people about the Irish weather and hunting foxes before going doolally.'

We wandered through the old farm things and moth-eaten animals with bits of their stuffing leaking out. It didn't take long to find the glass case with the stone in it. Shane saw it first.

'Wow!' he shouted. 'Look, Milo!'

Sure enough, there it was, sitting on a green velvet cloth. Shane took his stone from the bag and we compared it to the one in the case.

'It's a dead ringer for yours,' I said.

'It's part of it!' exclaimed Shane. 'Can't you see? If the two pieces were put together, the pattern would form complete circles. This is mega.'

On a plaque beside the display window there was a sign, which said:

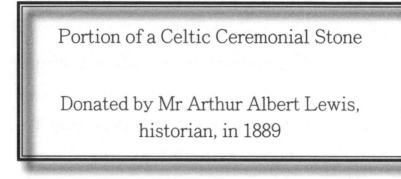

Portion of a Celtic Ceremonial Stone

Donated by Mr Arthur Albert Lewis,
historian, in 1889

Underneath there was more writing, but the words were covered by years of dust.

'That's him!' exclaimed Shane, practically dancing with wobbly excitement. 'See? I told you. That's the man who used to live in our house. If *this* bit of stone was in our garden, then *that* bit must have been there too.'

'Keep your voice down,' I said. 'We'll be thrown out.'

Too late.

A man with a frown attached to his hairy eyebrows was already making his way towards us. It was Mister Conway, keeper of the museum, wearing a dusty suit that fitted right in with the surroundings.

Shane shoved the stone into the takeaway bag before he could see it.

'What are you two up to?' Mister Conway asked.

'What makes you think we're up to anything?' said Shane. 'We only came to look at the old stuff.'

'None of your lip,' snapped Mister Conway. 'I've had my eye on you two.'

'Like, you think we came in to steal a rusty plough or a wormy butter churn?' said Shane.

'Ssshh, Shane,' I muttered, elbowing his tummy. 'Come on. We were just leaving anyway.' I pulled him after me down the front steps into the sunny street.

Shane couldn't stop talking about the two bits of stone. You'd think they were gold nuggets the way he was going on.

'They're just stones, Shane,' I said. 'So they were once stuck together, but they're still only bits of old stone with squiggly bits on them.'

There it was, that strange, tingly feeling again.

CHAPTER SIX

MILO HIDES THE STONE

Shane stopped when we got near his house. Big Ella was in the garden. Not weeding, because she said that every growing thing had a right to life; which was why the garden was a thick jungle. Shane shoved the takeaway bag into my hands.

'You take this, Milo,' he said. 'Gran would

have a fit if she thought I'd taken the stone.'

'What?' I said, backing away. 'You mean she didn't know you had it?'

'Well, you know Gran. She got vibes or something. She said she didn't want anyone to know about it because there'd be a fuss, like history nerds coming around the place with those little shovels you see them using on the History Channel. Nosing about and asking for tea and biscuits and taking stuff away.'

'Can't you pretend there's just school stuff in the bag?' I said.

Shane shook his head. 'She has X-ray eyes, my gran. Go on, just for a little while,' he pleaded. 'I'll phone you when the coast is clear and we'll put it back. What's the big deal?'

I gave a big *'you'll pay for this favour'* sigh

and took the bag. I quickly stuffed it into my schoolbag before my fingers could tingle again. Shane opened his squeaky gate.

'See you later,' he said with a wink.

I wasn't happy about being stuck with his crummy stone, not now that I knew about its past. But with Big Ella waving cheerfully at me, I couldn't very well start an argument. You don't do things like that to your best mate. So I waved back and went down to my own house. I hid that stone under the stairs. No way was I going to have it in my room.

★

Later on, when Mum was catching up on *Fair City* and *Coronation Street*, the phone rang in the hall.

'You get that, Milo. There's a love,' said Mum.

At first there was no reply to my 'hello' when I picked up the phone. There was a lot of background crackling and then the wheezy sound of someone breathing. Some saddo joker, I thought. Then I heard Shane's voice.

'Milo!' he cried.

'It's you!' I laughed. 'I might have known. What're you up to?'

'Milo! The stone!'

Such drama! 'OK, OK,' I said. 'No need to overact.'

'Milo …!' Shane's voice faded away.

I laughed when I put down the phone. I was well used to Shane and his huge dramas. He could just have asked me nicely to bring over the stone. But trust Shane to do his scary-voice thing. Still, I was glad to be getting rid of his old stone.

'Back in a while, Mum,' I called out, taking the bag from under the stairs. 'I'm just going over to Shane's.'

'Be back before dark,' Mum replied.

Well, that doesn't give me very long, I thought, as I pulled the front door shut. It was already dusk and all the neighbours' lights were on. All except one. I was surprised when I reached Shane's house and saw that it was in dusky darkness. Big Ella must have gone for a takeaway. Shane was probably lying in wait to pounce on me. Well, I'd be ready for him. But he didn't pounce. And there was no answer to the special knock Shane and I used whenever we called to one another's houses. By now his antics were getting right up my nose. 'I know you're there,' I called out through the letterbox. 'Come on, Shane, open up.'

I wasn't enjoying this creepiness. 'Stop acting the dork.' Then I laughed to myself when I realised that he was probably waiting for me at the stony place. I headed down the wild back garden.

'Ha!' I shouted when I saw the figure poking about the stones that Big Ella had dug up. 'You could have waited for me. You owe me at least a Crunchie for hanging on to this thing for you.'

The figure stopped and turned towards me. But it wasn't Shane. No, no. It definitely wasn't Shane. Even in that dim evening light, I could see the putty-coloured face and staring eyes of someone who didn't belong in this world.

CHAPTER SEVEN

DEEP, DEEP TROUBLE

We looked at one another for a few moments, him and me. The funny thing was, he seemed just as scared of me as I was of him.

So I said, 'Hello.'

He nodded and came towards me. I noticed his clothes. I'm not much into fashions — so long as I have the current Man United strip I don't much care what other people wear. But I could see that this guy was dressed like someone from one of those really old movies that you find on TV on a wet Sunday. Long coat, tall hat like a chimney pot, and hair that grew right down in front of his ears. Anyone, dead or alive, who went about like that could only be a harmless twit. Maybe. Hopefully.

'Who ... who are you?' I croaked. Not the most clever question, but cleverness doesn't really kick in when you're scared.

'Lewis. Deceased, as in dead,' the spook replied. 'Mister Arthur Albert Lewis to you, boy. And who are you?'

'Milo,' I said. 'Mister Milo Ferdinand Doyle to you.' I never ever tell anyone about the Ferdinand bit, but it seemed right just then. 'And what are you doing here? Are you the Lewis man who used to live here? The one who collected stones?'

'Ah, yes,' said Mister Arthur Albert Lewis, sitting down on one of Big Ella's dug-up stones. 'Well, Milo Ferdinand Doyle. We're in deep trouble here, sir. Deep, deep trouble.'

It was the 'we' part I didn't much like. So I sat down – near enough to hear what he was saying, but far enough to run if he made a spooky move in my direction.

Mister Lewis let out a sigh and leaned forward. 'It's to do with a special stone,' he went on.

Ah, I might have guessed. 'One with roundy patterns and a lizardy thing carved on it?' I asked.

He nodded very slowly and carefully, as one would, I suppose, if one was that ancient. And dead.

Mister Lewis looked at me with staring eyes. 'You know it?' he said.

'Sort of,' I replied, not adding that it was in the bag I was carrying. 'What about it?'

He gave another deep sigh. I wondered if spooks had lungs.

CHAPTER EIGHT

MISTER LEWIS'S STORY

'It's all to do with the ancient Celts,' Mister Lewis went on. 'That stone is a sacred stone that the Celts brought with them as they were chased across Europe by the Roman army. When the first Celts arrived here, they decided that Ireland would be the place to live.'

'They hadn't much choice,' I put in. 'This would have been the last bus stop after Europe. Any further and they'd have drowned in the Atlantic Ocean.'

Mister Lewis scowled. 'Don't interrupt, boy,' he said. 'This is serious.'

'Sorry,' I said. 'Go on.'

'Well, they made a ceremonial circle right here in the middle of Ireland, and their druid placed the stone in the centre. From then on, that stone was the most important thing to the Celts.'

'How do you know all this?' I asked.

'Because I'm a historian,' replied Mister Lewis grandly.

'*Was*,' I said.

'No need to remind me,' muttered Mister Lewis. 'Anyway, when I was digging here I discovered that stone — it was broken in two. Then I dug deeper and I discovered the remains of the stone circle. I could scarcely believe it.'

'How did you know what it was?'

Mister Lewis sniffed impatiently. 'Research, lad. That circle of stones went all around the nearby fields. When I realised its importance as a sacred place, I knew I'd have to cover it up and leave it in peace. So I bought any unusual stones from the farmers, at one penny each, to stop them being broken and scattered through ploughing or building. I thought if I simply buried them all together here I'd be doing a service to our ancestors. And yet ...' he paused and put his head in his hands. Not in a ghostly way like those pictures you see of spooks carrying their heads around damp castles. No, this was a worried head-in-hands thing. Just like you and me when there's a surprise maths test or a letter home from the school principal.

'And yet?' I prompted.

'And yet, as a historian, I felt I should pass part of my discovery on to heritage. So,' he paused again. 'So I buried one half of the circular stone. I gave the other half to the museum. I didn't say where I'd found it. I just made up a story about it.'

'In case there would be lots of history types coming here poking around?' I asked.

'Indeed,' said Mister Lewis. 'But it wasn't the history types who were to bother me,' he said. 'It was Celts and their druid.

'Huh?' I exclaimed. 'You mean one of those ancient guys in long frocks? Sort of like witchdoctors who scared people with their weird chanting and mad spells? Wow! I used to think druids were just made up. So druids were really real?'

Mister Lewis nodded. 'I should have known they'd come for the stone.' He sniffed and wiped his dead nose on his sleeve. 'Just like they've come for your friend and the big lady ...'

CHAPTER NINE

THE DRUID'S WARNING

I tried to say something else, but my tonsils had freaked out. I'd have done a runner right there and then except that my knees were locked with fear.

'That night, after I'd presented the half-stone to the museum,' Mister Lewis went on, 'I was sitting in my study when a great wind burst the door open, knocked my cocoa right out of my hand. Look,' he added, stretching out a skinny leg. 'You can still see the cocoa stains on my trousers. But then a figure emerged from the wind.'

'Who?' I whispered, looking about nervously. *Come on, knees, move!* But something about this sad spook made me want to know more. After all, my best mate was involved.

'Amergin,' replied Mister Lewis.

'Amergin? Should I know him?'

Mister Lewis shook his head. 'He was one of the first Irish druids,' he said. 'It was he who put the stone here originally. And he was very angry. Bloody angry, sir, if you'll pardon my forcefulness. Face like a bull in a rage.'

'Because the stone was broken?'

'No, it was because I had given away part of it. And that was the end of me,' he said with a sigh. 'I was ... er ... taken away. Deceased – but don't worry,' he went on as I fell off the stone I'd been sitting on. 'It didn't hurt,' he said. 'A quick demise – didn't really feel anything. No splutterings or gurgles or splashes of gore. Just a quiet draining of life from my head down through my toes.' He sighed and looked at his laced-up boots. 'My punishment was to guard this sacred place,' he went on. 'Not too bad until that scary woman started digging.'

'You've been here all those years?' I asked. 'All alone?'

'Here in this wilderness,' he replied. 'I wouldn't mind if there was a bit of a garden to sit in, like when other people lived here. But since that big lady came with her ecology-friendly madness, there's just all these weeds and dandelions. Look at them, lad. Talk about dreary! Why couldn't she just plant a few nice rosebushes and a flowery shrub or two, eh? Digging up the ancient stones, pah! Mad, interfering woman.'

Now was the time to sort all this. I had the solution. 'Tarra!' I said, lifting the tingly stone from the takeaway bag. I waited for Mister Lewis to dance — or have a happy float of joy with excitement, saying what a genius I was. He looked at the stone in my hand, but said nothing.

'It's the stone,' I prompted. 'The one that Shane took. Now he can come back, eh? Him and Big Ella?'

Mister Lewis shook his head. 'It's not that easy,' he said. 'When I said that Amergin was angry with me for separating the stone, that's nothing to what he is now with your friend and his granny. Now he's *really* angry. He's insisting that the two parts are to be put together and buried together.'

'Yeah? So why didn't you just spook your way into the museum and take the other half back?' I asked.

Mister Lewis snorted, then stuck back the bit of his nose that he'd snorted off. 'Hm,' he muttered, checking his nose carefully, 'Amergin keeps doing this to me. Sick joke. And look,' he went on, leaning across and putting his two hands around the stone I was holding. As he tried to lift it, it just stayed put. 'Ghostly hands,' he said. 'No grip.'

'I see,' I said. 'And ... and ... what about ...' my throat dried up again and I nodded towards the dark house.

'Your friends?' said Mister Lewis. 'Well,

that boy certainly stirred things up when he took the stone away. Until the two parts are united, the boy and his grandmother will end up like me, stuck in this draughty wilderness, minding a pile of stones for ever.'

'Are you saying that Shane and Big Ella are dead?' My heart kicked up. Would I never see my best mate again, except, perhaps, as a spook? Not able to share a bag of chips because he couldn't hold it, or kick a ball because his foot would go through it? Not much fun in that for Shane, even if it meant no homework.

'Not yet,' said Mister Lewis. 'Amergin has them. They're in a trance — a sort of sleep. The only way to save them from ending up like me is to get the rest of the stone from the museum and bury the two parts together.' Mr Lewis paused and then leant over and peered into my face. Whew, for a spook he had smelly breath and I really hoped all the bits of his face stayed put this time.

After a few moments of me staring up a spook's hairy nostril, he finally said, 'I need you to help me break into the museum.'

Oh great, I thought, just great. Now I was really scared. Chatting with a spook is one thing, but getting involved in breaking and entering was another. But, hey, my best mate and his gran were in trouble. I couldn't abandon them. I took a deep breath.

'OK,' I muttered, even though I was screaming inside.

'There will be a full moon tomorrow night,' said Mister Lewis, shaking his creaking head.

I wished he wouldn't do that. I so did not

want to see his head fall off.

'That's the time to do it,' he continued. 'This has to take place on the night of a full moon.'

'Why?'

'I don't know,' he said impatiently. 'I'm only going on what Amergin told me. Some ceremony or something, I suppose. They were fussy about the sun and the moon in those days.'

'So we only have tomorrow night to do this?' I said.

Mr Lewis's high hat wobbled as he nodded.

'What if we're late? What if we can't do this?'

'Then their bodies will be found next morning,' he sighed.

'No way!' I exclaimed. 'Mister Lewis, I couldn't live with myself if this didn't work out.'

'Well, you wouldn't live with yourself at all, my friend,' said Mister Lewis. 'Not now that you are part of all this.'

'What?' I croaked.

'You'd be dead too, young sir.'

CHAPTER TEN

OUT INTO THE NIGHT

It was dawn when I climbed through my bedroom window, exhausted and scared. I had intended to sneak into Dad's office and search the web to find out anything about Mister Lewis, but I crashed into bed and slept until I heard Mum shouting at me to get up. I wished I could tell her what was going on in the life of her only son, but where would you begin to tell your mum that you'd been hanging out with a dead person all night? So, looking normal on the outside and jittery as a green jelly on the inside, I sloped off to school.

Miss Lee tut-tutted when she saw Shane's empty desk.

'Anyone know if Shane is coming to school today?' she asked.

'I bet him and his gran are off mucking about with paint,' someone laughed.

Miss Lee smiled and shook her head as she marked Shane absent. Absent means 'not here', I thought. And, unless I put things right, not here ever again. I shut my eyes and wished him back here right now. But that was just being nerdy. So I opened my eyes again and thought about what I had to do.

I got through that day somehow. Even Mum was worried when I passed up on the ice-cream dessert and yummy sponge cake. And she reached for the thermometer when I said that I was taking an early night in bed.

'Just call me if you're feeling sick,' she said as she felt my forehead and tucked me in.

'Mum,' I said. 'I'm just a bit tired, that's all.'

How could I tell my mum that, if things didn't go right during the full moon, she'd never see me again? I'd be wafting about with Shane and Big Ella, looking in through windows, and longing for a spoonful of stew or a pancake.

I watched that moon cross my window. I could hear the comforting sound of the telly downstairs. Then the sounds of Dad locking up and Mum going to the bathroom. Then Dad singing off-key in the shower. Then silence.

The clock downstairs chimed ten forty-five. I had just fifteen minutes to meet spooky Mister Lewis in Shane's garden. I wanted to just curl up and hide. But my best friend and his gran were depending on me. With a sharp bite on my lip to get me going, I got up and put on my comforting old Bart Simpson leather (well, fake leather) jacket for good luck. Then I took my torch and the back-door key and crept out into the night.

'OK, Mister Lewis,' I whispered. 'Here I come.'

CHAPTER ELEVEN

BREAKING INTO BIG DANGER

Even though I was expecting him, I jumped when Mister Lewis loomed out of the long grass behind Shane's house.

'You sure look spooky,' I said with a shiver.

Mister Lewis frowned. 'What do you mean?' he asked crossly. 'Nothing has changed, except that I'm no longer alive.

I've always looked like this.'

'Oops, sorry!' I muttered. 'Maybe it's the hat.'

'Come along, young man,' went on Mister Lewis, leaving a slight breeze as he wafted through the long grass. 'And bring that stone with you,' he added, pointing to the takeaway bag I'd hidden behind the pile of stones the night before. 'I need to be absolutely sure the two pieces fit together.'

With a sigh, I shoved the stone inside my jacket and zipped up. I could feel it tingling against my ribs.

There weren't many people about on the street. I kept well back from Mister Lewis in case they'd think I was with a freaky guy. Until I realised they couldn't see him.

'How come ...?' I began.

'That nobody else can see me except you?'

Mister Lewis smiled and tapped his nose. 'It goes with the job,' he said. 'When I want to, I can be invisible. Though you caught me by surprise when you came to the stony place. Still, that's all for the good, now that you're helping.'

Not for my good, I thought.

★

Even with its big red door and the word 'Museum' in fancy writing over it, the building still had a creepy, empty look.

'How are we supposed to get in there?' I whispered.

Mister Lewis took off his hat and then straightened an ear that had come loose. He looked over the railings into the basement. Apart from a litter of Tayto crisp bags and squashed coke cans, there were just boarded-up windows.

'Let's try Chapel Lane,' said Mister Lewis, putting on his hat again.

This is too, too weird, I thought. I was still trying to get my head around the fact that I was following a dead man down a dark lane late at night to break into a museum. Hold that image and think how I felt.

Mister Lewis stopped in front of a small window high up.

'That will do, I think,' he said. 'That will be our way in.'

'Huh?' I said. 'How do I get up there?'

Mister Lewis tut-tutted, and shook his head.

'Do you have to be so negative, Milo, my boy?' He pointed to a wheelybin. 'Tarra, as you say yourself. Pull it over here and you can climb up. All you'll have to do then is smash that window. Easy.'

CHAPTER TWELVE

ALARM BELLS

I looked at the small window. I had never broken a window before. Well, yes I had, but not on purpose, you understand.

'For heaven's sake, get a move on,' hissed Mister Lewis, looking around nervously.

'It's OK,' I retorted. 'Nobody uses this laneway. It only leads to the river and nobody will be using it at this time of night.'

'It's not people I'm worried about,' said

Mister Lewis. 'It's the time.' He looked around again as the town-hall clock chimed the half hour. 'We only have until midnight.'

'Oh blast!' I swore. I looked at the window again and unzipped my jacket.

'What are you doing?' asked Mister Lewis.

'Putting this to good use,' I said, taking the stone out and wrapping it in the jacket.

'Just don't damage it,' warned Mister Lewis.

He was right. If the stone was broken some more, then this Amergin guy would certainly lose his cool. But in a freaky situation like this, you have to take chances.

I dragged the wheelybin over to the wall and climbed up on to the roof of the built-on annexe beneath the museum window. With a 'stand clear', I swung the stone and smashed it against the window.

The first blow just bounced. I swung the jacket again. This time there was a loud tinkling of glass as the window shattered. Without waiting to find out if we'd been heard, I used the stone in the jacket to clear away the sharp bits that were left. The stone shuddered for just a moment, but it stayed intact.

What was I thinking? I really wanted to go home and lie down. Mister Lewis puffed and panted as he climbed up after me, making me wonder again about ghostly lungs. Then he squeezed through the narrow window and jumped down beside me into the dark museum.

'I thought you'd be able to waft through,' I whispered as I put on my jacket again, and noticed, in the light from the street light outside, that Bart Simpson's face was hanging off. But I had greater things to worry about. I stuffed the stone inside and zipped up. 'What sort of a spook are you if you can't go through walls?'

'Don't be difficult, Milo, my man,' said Mister Lewis.'It's not all wafting and floating, you know. Besides, I'm only a half-ghost.'

'Sshh,' I hissed.

'What?'

'I'm listening for a burglar alarm.'

'Pardon me?'

'Burglar alarm.' I said. 'It sets off bells. Computer alarm,' I added, to let him know how advanced the world had become since his day, hoping he wouldn't ask me how it worked.

But there were no alarm bells. Anyway, I thought, who'd want to steal anything from here?

'Come on,' I whispered, switching on my torch and leading the way to the showcase where the other half of the stone was displayed.

Mister Lewis's face lit up, as much as a ghostly face can; it went from being white, putty coloured, to a pale beige like my granny's stockings.

'Oh my goodness,' he breathed. 'There it is, just as I presented it.'

'You should have left it in the ground,' I muttered.

'I know, I know,' said Mister Lewis sadly, making me sorry for him. After all, even half-ghosts have feelings too.

'Never mind, Mister Lewis,' I went on. 'We'll have that back with its other half in seconds.'

'Before you do anything, Master Milo

Ferdinand,' said Mister Lewis, grandly. 'Would you mind wiping the dust off that sign there?'

'Sure.' I took a used tissue from my pocket and rubbed the sign. The dust lifted from the placard and Mister Lewis bent down and peered at the words. 'My, my,' he said. 'So that's how I died! I had no idea. You never really remember your death, you know. Not that I'm fully dead,' he added ruefully.

I looked over his shoulder at the words on the bottom of the sign.

'"*Tragically and mysteriously killed by a falling stone that struck him on the head*",' I read. 'Did Amergin do that?' I asked nervously. 'Clobbered you with one of his ancient stones?'

Mister Lewis sighed. 'I stirred up things

with a stone, so it seems right I should die by a stone. Didn't see it coming, though.'

I swallowed hard. So, was that the fate that was in store for me and Shane and Big Ella? Knocked on the head by a Celtic druid with a hunk of stone? I shivered.

'Let's get on with this,' I said. I kicked the glass case. It shattered quite easily. And that's when the bells started clanging.

CHAPTER THIRTEEN

MISTER LEWIS FINDS A NEW TALENT

'What's that? What's happening?' shouted Mister Lewis, his ghostly hands pressed over his ears.

'It's the alarm!' I cried. 'Come on, we've got to get out of here.'

I reached in and grabbed the half stone from the shattered showcase, zipped it inside my jacket along with the other half. We ran between the other showcases, the two stones rattling together against my chest. When we reached the high window that we'd come through I stopped. There was a face at the broken window. And a voice I recognised. 'Sergeant Johnson!' I whispered, ducking under a showcase. Too late, he'd seen me.

'You, boy,' he shouted angrily, flashing his torch around. 'What do you think you're doing? I can see your legs. No point in hiding, the place is surrounded. You might as well give yourself up.'

'Surrounded?' muttered Mister Lewis. 'Oh dear.'

'Surrounded by him,' I whispered. 'There's always only one Garda on night duty. I should know – my dad is a Garda and he's on night duty every third week.'

Still, we'd have to risk going out through the museum door. But as we edged along the wall towards it, I was horrified to hear a key in the lock and bolts being pulled back. We were trapped! I frantically looked around the moonlit room for a hiding place. There was a Famine display of a life-size group of people sitting at a fake fire. I crept over and nicked a bit of sacking from a donkey cart and put it around my shoulders to look raggy. Then I sat beside a model of a boy whose paint-chipped hand was stretched towards the fire. I ducked lower when a beam from a torch flashed around. It was only a matter of moments before I'd be seen.

'Who's there?' came an angry shout. I can never understand why people ask that question at a time like this. Like, someone who's broken in is going to stand up and give his name, address and mobile number and say *'take me away'*? Anyway, I gasped when I recognised Mister Conway's voice. I'd forgotten he lived upstairs. He'd heard us!

'Do something,' I hissed at Mister Lewis, who was sitting across from me, his tall hat askew, making him look like a worn-out scarecrow.

'Do what?' he hissed back.

'Something ghostly. I'll be in no end of trouble if I'm caught.'

If I did get caught, then I wouldn't get to replace the two bits of stone, and Shane and Big Ella would be found dead in the morning. And me — found dead in a prison cell because Amergin, being a full spook, could just walk through the wall and clobber me. And my dad would be kicked out of the Gardaí and jailed for – I dunno – for having a criminal son, maybe. And Mum would have to leave the country in disgrace with a wig and a false passport. Such worries!

The beam of the torch was coming closer. I shut my eyes and held my breath as it stopped and then passed over me. Then there was a sound that startled me.

'OOooo.'

I blinked. Mister Lewis was now standing beside a model of an old woman who was stirring something in a pot. His head was raised and he was uttering this ghastly wail. The beam of torchlight stopped, then focused on the display.

'OoooooOO,' went Mister Lewis, now in full cry.

'Help!' bawled Mister Conway. 'Help!' He stood frozen to the spot. With a clatter, the door burst open and Sergeant Johnson barged in.

'Mister Conway!' he exclaimed. 'Have you caught the hooligans?'

'Sergeant,' said Mister Conway nervously. 'There's something ...'

'What, man, what? Are they armed and dangerous?'

'Over there,' whispered Mister Johnson. 'That old woman ...'

Sergeant Johnson shone his torch on the group. I sucked in my cheeks and hoped I looked hungry enough to be a Famine kid.

'They're models, man,' he said, 'just Famine models.'

'She ooohhhed at me,' whispered Mister Conway.

'Huh? Don't be ridiculous,' began Sergeant Johnson.

Mister Lewis launched into another wail.

Sergeant Johnson jumped. 'What the blazes?' he shouted, clutching Mister Conway's arm, even though Mister Conway was already hanging on to Sergeant Johnson's collar.

'OOOOooo,' went Mister Lewis again. Then he changed position and slipped behind a hairy model of a donkey. 'EEEEHAAAWW,' he went.

Sergeant Johnson shone his torch in the direction of the donkey.

'EEEHAAAWWW!'

'See?' shouted Mister Conway in panic. 'It's haunted!'

I could see the glee in Mister Lewis's face as he wafted towards the two men. He turned and winked at me. He was visible to me and invisible to them. Neat trick. Then he shrieked louder than ever into their ears. That did it. The two men ran, tripping over one another. Mister Lewis followed them, screeching all the time. The door slammed and I could hear the clatter of panicky footsteps running into the street. Mister Lewis wafted back to me. He was laughing loudly as he wiped ghostly tears from his eyes with his sleeve and stuck back an eyebrow.

'That was wonderful,' he said. 'Best fun I've ever had in my life. Eh, I mean death,' he added. 'I didn't know I could shriek like that. Think of the fun I could have had all those years I've spent as a half-ghost. Come on, Milo. Let's chase those two and maybe a few more passers-by for a laugh, eh?'

'No way!' I said. 'Have you forgotten why we're doing all this? Come on, we've got to get out of here before they come back with back-up.'

'Yes, of course,' said Mister Lewis, suddenly ghostly serious again. 'It must be nearly midnight.'

That made me panic again. Luckily I hadn't had dinner. I'd have thrown up right there on the museum floor – and if the cops didn't get me, then forensics would. I've seen those guys on the telly – nailing a thug from just a splash of sneezed snot on a doorhandle.

CHAPTER FOURTEEN

AN UNFORTUNATE ENCOUNTER

Keeping well in the shadows, I slipped along Main Street, the two stones rattling against my ribs. So far so OK. But when I looked around there was no sign of Mister Lewis! Had he deserted me? Had Amergin come early and swept him away? It was all too much. I couldn't call out. I just wanted to lie down and cover my head, but I knew I totally had to keep going to try to sort out Big Ella and Shane by myself. At any moment, I expected to feel Amergin's icy fingers around my neck, or else hear the *wee-waa* sound of the cop car. It was tempting to go back and give myself up — after all, cops are human. But then I thought of Shane and Big Ella and I kept on going. I got as far as the Bella Patata chip shop.

A couple of guys were hassling Alberto, the owner, who was trying to close up for the night. There was nobody else on the street at this late hour to help him. You've probably guessed who they were. Yep, none other than Wedge and Crunch! Now I really wished I'd been caught and was locked up safely in a cell. Even Amergin wafting through the cell bars to finish me off would be better than being caught by those two. Then they spotted me.

'Well, if it isn't Nerdy Milo,' one of them laughed. The two of them switched their attention to me. I tried to ignore them and kept walking, but I should have known better. They got in front of me and crowded me so that I couldn't pass.

'Out so late?' sneered Crunch.

'Does your mummy know you're out on the street?' asked Wedge, pushing his face right up to mine.

'Don't hassle me,' I said, backing away. Like, I needed this confrontation right now? Time was so scarce!

'Or you'll put manners on us?' laughed Crunch.

'No,' I said, thinking so fast my brain was amazed. 'Because I'm psychic. I have dead friends who'll come and get you.'

The two bullies laughed. I pressed my arms tighter around the stones in my jacket, hoping they wouldn't notice the bulge and dump the stones in the river.

'You little liar,' snarled Crunch. 'Let's see what you're hiding there.' He put out his hand to open the zip. That was as far as he got. To my great relief, I heard a familiar sound coming from just beside Wedge's ear.

'OooOOOOOOOOoo!'

Mister Lewis! I'd have hugged him if I could have seen where he was.

'I'm coming for you, boy. Back from the dead. Mend your wicked ways. OooOOOOoo!'

With a wail, Wedge raced away. Crunch stopped trying to open my jacket and looked at me. 'How did you do that, you little worm ...?'

With a swoop, Mister Lewis was at his side.

'OooOOOOoo,' he wailed into Crunch's ear. 'Bad, bad boy. You must come with meee. I have a nice burial chamber just for yooouu.'

Nice burial chamber? Cool! I had to laugh.

Crunch looked at me, his face ghastly white in the street light.

'Told you,' I said. 'You want to watch it, you creep. That's my dead pal. With fangs,' I added as an extra.

That was enough for Crunch; he was off like a rabbit from a greyhound. Mister Lewis laughed. 'I've never had such fun,' he said as he loomed into sight again.

'Right,' I grunted. 'But it's held us back! Where were you?'

'I, er, went back to give another little scare to those two men,' he confessed. 'Just a little bit of fun … I've never had fun. Ever.'

'Yeah, well this is not the time for being jolly. I was the one who was scared,' I muttered. 'Come on. Some friend you are!'

'Friend, Milo? You call me friend?'

I looked up at him as we ran. His face looked like a warmed-up omelette, and he was smiling.

'Yeah. My best spook friend. Now, come on, we've work to do.'

As we made our way up the street, there was another wail. This time it really was the wail of a police car speeding by.

'Sergeant Johnson must have phoned the next town for back-up,' I laughed. With a quick glance behind, I was pleased to see it chasing after Crunch and Wedge as they raced past the museum. They'd be spending the rest of the night answering questions about the break-in. Good. That meant that the Gardaí wouldn't be searching the streets for a while.

The two stones rattled under my torn jacket as I ran. The streets became a blur. It was such a lonely, frightening feeling. As we got near to our road, I was so tempted to head for my own house, tear upstairs and throw myself into my parents' room and beg for protection.

'Mum, Dad!' I'd shout as I leapt on their bed with the rattling stones. 'Me and a dead man are being chased by druids who have Shane and Big Ella prisoners. Help!'

Nah. I brushed that image from my worn-out mind. Dad would grunt and mutter, and Mum would offer to get me a nice cup of drinking chocolate to soothe my nightmare.

And then the Town Hall clock began to chime. Midnight!

CHAPTER FIFTEEN

THE MIDNIGHT RUSH

The scary hour had come! Now I really *did* want to turn back, but forced myself to run even faster towards Shane and Big Ella's house, Mister Lewis wafting beside me, urging me to hurry.

'It's OK for you,' I panted, 'but I have real legs that don't waft like yours.' Not yet, anyway!

We'd just got as far as Big Ella's gate when the clock stopped chiming midnight.

'Shane!' I called out as I ran past the house and down towards the stony place. 'Shane!'

I almost fell down when I saw the shadowy figures standing in a half circle. And there, before them, were Shane and Big Ella. They were totally still, like in a trance. One of the shadowy figures broke away and moved towards them.

'That's Amergin,' whispered Mister Lewis, his voice shaky with fear.

'The stones!' I said, pulling the two stone halves from inside my jacket. 'I have them.'

Mister Lewis shook his head. 'Too late, lad,' he said. 'No good now. Midnight has passed. All is lost.'

I watched, terrified, as Amergin moved. I couldn't see his face. He wore long clothes and had long hair that wafted about like a dirty cobweb. At a signal from him, the rest of the ghostly shapes also began to move towards Shane and Big Ella.

'They're going to turn them into half-ghosts – just like me,' groaned Mister Lewis. 'They're doomed!'

That's when I got really angry. I was not going to stand by and watch my best mate and his gran made into spooks.

'Stop!' I shouted, running into the circle. Shane and Big Ella were kneeling, their heads bent forward, like they were still in a trance.

'Get away from my friends, you creeps!' I roared.

Amergin drifted towards me. I could see his face now, all right, and it was not pretty. He had mad eyes that would bore holes in a skyscraper. His voice shook the ground and made my bones tremble. I didn't understand what he was saying. Terrified and angry, I yelled back at him, any rubbish I could think of to disguise my terror. His deep, earthquaky voice got louder. And then Mister Lewis was beside me. He was trying to pull me away, except that his hands kept going through me.

'Don't upset him, lad,' he whispered.

But I wasn't listening. I ripped off my jacket and hurled it, and the two stone halves, at Amergin.

'There's your crummy stones,' I shouted. 'We went to awful trouble to get them – me and Mister Lewis. And you can keep the jacket!' I added, kicking it towards Amergin. Then I rushed over to Shane and Big Ella.

'Get them out of their trance,' Mister

Lewis's voice shouted from behind.

I don't know what I was thinking, but that was when I pushed Big Ella on top of Shane. She was a big lady and she squashed him like a frog under a tractor. If Amergin didn't kill him, then Big Ella certainly would.

'I've killed my best friend,' was my last thought before the circle of foggy shapes began to close in and everything went black.

CHAPTER SIXTEEN

MISTER LEWIS TELLS ALL

When I woke up, I was lying in the long grass behind Shane's house. It was still dark. I looked around in terror, expecting to see those spooks looming again. But there was nobody. Was it over? Was I dead? I kicked at a rock, expecting my foot to go through it. It didn't.

'Ouch!' I yelped.

'What did you do that for?' It was Mister Lewis. He floated towards me, still a spook.

'I thought I might be dead,' I replied.

'Dead?' he laughed. 'Not at all, my dear friend.'

'But what happened?' I asked. 'What about Shane and Big Ella?'

'They're back at the house,' said Mister Lewis. 'They're safe. Look, my dear, brave Master Milo Ferdinand, I don't have much time. I just want to thank you.'

'Huh?'

'For getting me away from this dreary place. Shush, listen,' he went on as I started to ask questions. 'You want to know what happened out here? I'll tell you. I can only stay a few moments.'

'Why?' I asked.

'Because I have a ticket to go somewhere better than this stony dump,' he said with a smile. 'When you pushed the big lady on to her grandson, it was the best move you'll ever make in your life.'

'But wasn't Amergin very angry with me?' I said.

Mister Lewis shook his head. 'I thought so too,' he admitted. 'But then I heard a sound that I thought I'd never, ever hear.' He paused, smiling at whatever he was remembering.

'Yeah? Go on.'

'It was the sound of Amergin laughing,' he said. 'Can you imagine? A powerful Celtic druid laughing. His whole body – at least his whole ghostly body – was shaking with laughter at the sight of Big Ella flattening her grandson. I haven't laughed so much myself since … since … oh, to tell the truth, I just never, ever laughed like that.'

'Really?' I said. 'He actually laughed? The great Amergin?'

'It really was amusing,' said Mister Lewis. 'And then he sent away the circle of druids and indicated to Big Ella to haul the lad back to the house.'

'So, Shane never saw what went on?' I asked.

'No. He won't remember any of this. You must not tell him.'

I didn't quite agree. What was the point in going through all this stuff and not being able to chat to Shane about it? And make sure he'd always be grateful to me for the rest of time? But I nodded. I'd have agreed to anything because I was alive, and so were my best mate and his gran.

'I must go now,' went on Mister Lewis. He smiled again and rubbed his spooky hands together. 'I'm all done here,' he said. 'My stone-guarding duties are over. The stone halves have been joined together and buried and,' he smiled, 'Amergin has freed me.'

'To go where?' I asked again.

Mister Lewis winked and shrugged his dusty shoulders. 'That's what I have to find out. But it has to be a better place than this dreary wasteland. It's been great to meet you. So, goodbye, Milo, my friend.'

He held out his hand and I took it. It was surprisingly warm. At least, it left a warm feeling in my own hand and in my heart. In an instant, Mister Lewis was gone.

'Goodbye, you old spook,' I whispered. 'I hope you'll find harps and sunshine and get to dance on fluffy clouds.'

There were lights downstairs in Shane's house. I pushed open the back door. Big Ella was in the kitchen. She was painting a huge canvas. At this hour? How mad was this?

'Milo!' she said. 'Mister Lewis told me to leave you alone, that he'd look after you.'

'What are you doing?' I asked. This was getting even crazier.

'I'm doing what Amergin asked me to do,' she laughed as she splashed on another swish with her paintbrush. 'I'm painting a picture of the stone. That's what he wants. He said it was so that people will never forget our ancient history.'

'Where did he go, him and those other guys in frocks?' I asked.

'Amergin took the stones, still wrapped in

whatever you'd put around them,' said Big Ella. 'And they all simply disappeared. Just me and that nice Mister Lewis left. What a pity he didn't call years ago. We could have chatted over tea and muffins …'

'Where is Shane?' I put in.

She nodded towards the ceiling. 'He's upstairs, asleep. Wow, he's some weight!'

She suddenly looked serious. 'He mustn't know about tonight's events, Milo,' she said. 'He couldn't cope with all that's happened. Mister Lewis promised me that Shane won't remember any of it. You and I are the only ones who know what went on here tonight. Now, how's about a warm muffin to help you get back to normal before you go home, eh?

'Normal?' I said. 'What's normal, Big Ella?' Could I ever be normal after all this?

CHAPTER SEVENTEEN

SWIRLING COLOURS AND ROUNDY DESIGNS

'Let's go to the museum,' Shane said, after school a week later.

'What?' I said. 'Why do you want to go there? We were there last week.'

'I want to see it again.'

'Oh, all right,' I groaned. I'd had it up to my tonsils with druids and circles-inside-circles, thank you very much.

At the beginning of the alley I stopped to shake a stone from my shoe. Shane was still chatting to himself, didn't even know I'd stopped. When I caught up with him around the corner he had company. Yes, it was my night-time pals, Crunch Kelly and Wedge Murphy. They were hassling Shane. They had him pressed against a wall, one searching his pockets, the other trying to steal Shane's new runners. I watched for just a couple of seconds.

'Run!' Shane yelled at me. 'Get away from these scumbags!'

That was my best pal – watching out for me. But now it was my turn. I sauntered towards them.

'Excuse me, boys,' I said.

It was Crunch who saw me first. I smiled, and he froze. He tapped Wedge who was stooped down, untying the second runner.

'What?' Wedge said impatiently. 'Can't you see I'm busy, Crunch?'

Then he looked up and saw me. 'Woooo,' I whispered. 'Been in court yet, boys?' They both looked around frantically and, holding on to each other, they scarpered.

Shane's mouth opened wide. 'Hey, Milo,' he said. 'How did you do that?'

I tapped my nose. 'I got that trick from a friend,' I said. 'A very old friend,' I added.

'Liar, liar, pants on fire,' said Shane. 'We go way back, I know everyone you know …'

'Maybe not everyone,' I said. 'Now, come on. Let's see what's happening.'

There was a crowd in the museum. Mister

Conway was there, like a demented general with piles, fussing and telling people to get in line. Shane and I ducked our way to the centre of the attraction.

'I'm so proud,' whispered Shane.

And so he should be. His gran's painting of the druidstone had everyone excited. The swirling colours and roundy designs were simply magic. Celtic magic. The museum people had bought the picture for permanent display in the newly done-up glass case where the half druidstone had been.

'This painting is extremely valuable now that the druidstone has been stolen by robbers,' Mister Conway was saying to the crowd. How would he react if I told him that the robbers were me and the dead Mister Albert Arthur Lewis!

'OooOOOoo!' I couldn't resist, could I?

Mister Conway ducked down and put his hands on his head.

'Eh, I think I dropped me, eh, keys,' he muttered when he came up for air. He blushed and ran his eyes over all of us. Just for an instant he focused on me, and then glanced over at the Famine scene. Then he shook his head, probably to shake away that night and stop himself from associating living faces with the whole spooky thing.

'Just think, Milo,' said Shane when we went outside, 'the council arc having cards and calendars and prints and stuff done from that painting by my gran. They say it'll bring tourists to liven up our town. By the way,' he continued, taking something from his pocket. 'I found this in the long grass behind our house. Didn't you have a jacket with this on it?'

I looked at the tatty little bit of the jacket with Bart Simpson's face on it, and I smiled.

'Not any more,' I said. 'It was nicked by a druid.'

'Yeah, right,' laughed Shane. 'Like, he wore it to Grace O'Malley's tea party!'

'Sure thing,' I smiled.

**COMING SOON
MORE MILO ADVENTURES**

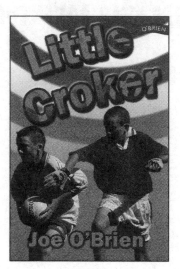

Little Croker

Danny Wilde wants one thing more than anything else
in the world and that's to get his GAA team, Littlestown
Crokes, to the top of the League.
But when things go horribly wrong, can they make it
after all?